P9-CDM-950

Baa, Baa, Black Sheep

and

Baa, Baa, Pink Sheep

Retold by Mick Gowar
Illustrated by O'Kif

Crabtree Publishing Company

www.crabtreebooks.com

Crabtree Publishing Company
www.crabtreebooks.com
1-800-387-7650

PMB 59051, 350 Fifth Ave.
59th Floor,
New York, NY 10118

616 Welland Ave.
St. Catharines, ON
L2M 5V6

Published by Crabtree Publishing in 2012
Printed in the U.S.A./052012/FA20120413

Series editor: Jackie Hamley
Editor: Kathy Middleton
Proofreader: Reagan Miller
Series advisor: Dr. Hilary Minns
Series designer: Peter Scoulding
Production coordinator and
   Prepress technician: Margaret Amy Salter
Print coordinator: Katherine Berti

Text (Baa, Baa, Pink Sheep)
© Mick Gowar 2008
Illustration © O'Kif 2008

The rights of Mick Gowar to be
identified as the author of Baa,
Baa, Pink Sheep and O'Kif as
the illustrator of this Work have
been asserted.

The author and publisher would
like to thank Frances Gowar for
permission to reproduce the
photograph on p. 14.

First published in 2008
by Franklin Watts
(A division of Hachette
Children's Books)

**Library and Archives Canada
Cataloguing in Publication**

Gowar, Mick, 1951-
    Baa baa, black sheep, and Baa baa, pink sheep
/ retold by Mick Gowar ; illustrated by O'Kif.

(Tadpoles: nursery rhymes)
Issued also in electronic format.
ISBN 978-0-7787-7883-7 (bound).--
ISBN 978-0-7787-7895-0 (pbk.)

    1. Nursery rhymes, English. I. O'Kif II. Title.
III. Series: Tadpoles (St. Catharines, Ont.). Nursery
rhymes

PZ8.3.G69Ba 2012   j398.8   C2012-902467-8

**Library of Congress
Cataloging-in-Publication Data**

CIP available at Library of Congress

Baa, Baa, Black Sheep

O'Kif

"I remember when my children were very little. I read them rhymes or counted sheep until they went to sleep. Although, sometimes, I fell asleep first!"

Baa, baa, black sheep,

have you any wool?

Yes sir, yes sir,
three bags full.

One for the master,

and one for the dame.

One for the little boy
who lives down the lane.

Baa, Baa, Black Sheep

Baa, baa, black sheep,
have you any wool?
Yes sir, yes sir,
three bags full.

One for the master,
and one for the dame.
One for the little boy
who lives down the lane.

Can you point to the
rhyming words?

Baa, Baa, Pink Sheep

Mick Gowar

"This is me in my shed. This is where I write my books. When I'm not writing, I like visiting schools to read my books and tell stories to the children."

Baa, baa, pink sheep,
have you any wool?

No sir, no sir,
none at all.

None for the master,

and none for the dame.

None for the little boy who shivers down the lane.

21

Baa, Baa, Pink Sheep

Baa, baa, pink sheep,
have you any wool?
No sir, no sir,
none at all.

None for the master,
and none for the dame.
None for the little boy
who shivers down the lane.

Can you point to the
rhyming words?

Puzzle Time!

Which of the things on this page are made of wool?

Notes for adults

TADPOLES NURSERY RHYMES are structured for emergent readers.
The books may also be used for read-alouds or shared reading with young children.

The language of nursery rhymes is often already familiar to an emergent reader. Seeing the rhymes in print helps build phonemic awareness skills. The alternative rhymes extend and enhance the reading experience further, and encourage children to be creative with language and make up their own rhymes.

IF YOU ARE READING THIS BOOK WITH A CHILD, HERE ARE A FEW SUGGESTIONS:

1. Make reading fun! Choose a time to read when you and the child are relaxed and have time to share the story.

2. Recite the nursery rhyme together before you start reading. What might the alternative rhyme be about? Brainstorm ideas.

3. Encourage the child to reread the rhyme and to retell it using his or her own words. Invite the child to use the illustrations as a guide.

4. Help the child identify the rhyming words when the whole rhymes are repeated on pages 12 and 22. This activity builds phonological awareness and decoding skills. Encourage the child to make up alternative rhymes.

5. Give praise! Children learn best in a positive environment.

IF YOU ENJOYED THIS BOOK, WHY NOT TRY ANOTHER TITLE FROM TADPOLES: NURSERY RHYMES?

Hey Diddle Diddle and Hey Diddle Doodle   978-0-7787-7884-4 RLB   978-0-7787-7896-7 PB
Humpty Dumpty and Humpty Dumpty at Sea   978-0-7787-7885-1 RLB   978-0-7787-7897-4 PB
Itsy Bitsy Spider and Itsy Bitsy Beetle   978-0-7787-7886-8 RLB   978-0-7787-7898-1 PB

VISIT WWW.CRABTREEBOOKS.COM FOR OTHER CRABTREE BOOKS.

Answers